# Little Indiscretions

M.C. Gardner

*MC 2020*

# M.C. GARDNER

She is the author of several books of verse and short stories. She is an essayist and translator for international magazines. Her poems and short stories have been included in many anthologies and collections. Some of her short stories were written during creative writing sessions in the South-East of England.

Elias, Dip to his nearest and dearest was born on the shores of Lake Tahoe while his mother was taking a family holiday from Scotland. It was a hot Monday afternoon. The miracle happened at 3.25pm.

His prosperous family of Huguenot ancestry did not welcome him with open arms as he was no.8 on a scale of 9 brothers and one stubborn and annoying little sister with very high IQ.

His early life went on uneventful, primary school in his little town of 150 souls on the Borders of which were all members of his own close family, to which one should add two sets of grandparents dedicated to birdwatching, uncles and aunts, bullying cousins who made the number.

His father, an astronomer emeritus at the University of Edinburgh, who was in residence there twice a week for bespoke lectures and one tutorial, sent him to a boarding school near Aberdeen, to get him out of the provincial life and to make him less clingy to the resident sheep which were grazing on the family land.

He never came back home from Aberdeen, spending his holidays with his father's sister who was married to a banker and learning how to behave upper-class!

Dip got a scholarship to study classics and divinity at the University of St Andrews. On the day he was due to be ordained, he eloped with Myfanwy, a healthy lass from Wales, a former President of the Debating Society who was a law graduate and who was preparing to become a Barrister.

This forced him to join the local police and from there he rose through the ranks to become a superintendent.

When he retired, and with time on his hands - when his wife did not require his domestic skills - he began to write his Diary. Myfanwy suggested putting it on line. The literary editor of The Universe happened to discover it after one night of heavy drinking. Hooked, he contacted Dip's publishers, who, grasping the opportunity of making money, were quick to contact Dip, who became an overnight sensation, with offers from some well-known publishers.

Dip is an early riser. His four short-haired, non-pedigree cats have to be brushed and fed first. He makes himself a cup of coffee from sustainable plantations – Myfanwy insists.

He does not sit at his desk to write, because he has nothing to write about at the beginning of the day.

From their bespoke kitchen he can hear Myfanwy in her bedroom with Laura Ashley wall-paper with cranes and tulips.

'Dip, where are you?'

Diligently, Dip rushes upstairs with the coffee, a bowl of organic cereals, a jug of almond milk, and a bowl of mixed blueberries, raspberries and blackberries, not strawberries because Myfanwy does not like them.

'Dip, Uncle Charlie will be visiting us as from tomorrow. You'll need to get the blue bedroom ready, and make sure you take down Aunt Maureen's portrait. Put it in the attic, out of sight! And I mean it!'

'And why is that? I thought, after Aunt Maureen's demise he went to Oz for good.'

'Apparently, he has recharged his batteries and he is back.'

'Myfanwy, it cannot be…in the dating game? Wasn't she the love of his life?'

'Difficult to say now. Yes, in his past. Aunt Maureen was, but now? He will be staying as long as it takes to – he informed me in his e-mail sent to me 15 mins. ago - that he has made an appointment to consult a spiritualist.'

'What? Why is that? You are having me on!'

'Stop interrupting! He has met this woman, half his age, who is big in birdwatching circles in the Blue Mountains. He is head over hills…'

'The old git!'

'I forbid you to refer to my Uncle Charlie in this manner! He has asked for a séance to check if late Aunt Maureen is in agreement with this change in his life!'

'Myfanwy, you surprise me! Your Uncle Charlie is a professor of physics.'

'Dip, you are so simple, there are unexplained things even for a scientist like him! No wonder they retired you! It's not the middle ages! Uncle Charlie wants to know if his intended is truthful in her intentions!'

'This is what we need now! Can't he go to a hotel and then rent an apartment?'

'Dip, no time for chatting! I have an urgent case at the Courts. Here is the list of domestic duties for today. You can leave me now.'

Dip says nothing; he is ready to go for a game of golf with his former Chief. Then it is elevenses and gossip at the mother-in-law's over the road.

He usually drives her into town, except on Tuesdays and Wednesdays when he works at the police station.

Today he has lunch with his publisher.

Fish and salad, no dressing, because Myfanwy forbids it. It's her latest organic diet as she believes Dip is getting geriatric by the day.

In the afternoon, he goes for a walk in the park, and then he does some digging in the garden. By teatime, Myfanwy is back, in a right mood as the Judge has rescheduled the trial.

'I am dining with my colleagues. It's the Head of the Chambers' birthday. No spouses.'

Dip makes himself a cup of tea and a crumpet with mango preserve.

He watches the news and then he sits himself at his study. His cats snore softly next to him. He opens his laptop and he begins to write today's entry.

*Monday*

A sunny day to start, which developed into a sticky drizzle.

Today has been a trying one. In the morning, I got the letter from the Planning Office. They refused planning permission for an extension at the back of the house. Their reason was that it would create a shadow over the neighbour's garage.

I wonder if it was wise for me to retire. I shall submit the same plans, this time for an extension at the front, though it's going to put half the street in shadow!

Lunch was a modest affair: cheese on eggs. It's all Myfanwy's fault. She insisted on working part-time, three times a week. I caught up with a few programmes on TV. Super. Those mediaeval men knew a thing or two about defence. I immersed myself in culture. Myfanwy keeps telling me that my job has brutalised me and that I've lost all my pre-marriage sensibility. She can talk from her hobby as a professional wrestler!

Myfanwy came home late again. I wonder what kept her so late. Perhaps I should investigate. As soon as she came home, she changed into her running gear and was off for a long run - she tells me that she has entered the London marathon again!

I fell asleep in my armchair. As Myfanwy was taking her time, I went to bed on my own. Anyway she insists on separate bedrooms as she says it ignites the feelings and saves me from her snoring!

*Tuesday*

Myfanwy was long gone after I got up late. Listened to the weather forecast. Still nice weather until the end of the week. I shall hoe the garden, sprinkle some rose fertiliser and do some serious watering as the lawn is drying out.

The immediate neighbour on the right, who moved in last week, keeps sunning herself in the garden. She might have a night job! But what? A young lass like her should have a job. I have not seen a partner there.

Had lunch alone in front of the TV set. It was dragging on about Europe. Unwisely, the PM has opened a can of worms, or a "Pandora's Box" as the newsreader expressed it more politely! It has divided the country right down the middle. I am glad I retired.

The neighbour, in a bikini, rang the bell and introduced herself as Francesca. She asked me to her house for coffee. I went straightaway and I learnt that she and her partner have started work at the local hospital. They are both nurses, but they have been scheduled for different shifts.

She offered me the worst coffee which was on a par with the one from the station. She is from Wales and they have four tomcats, all castrated. She referred to them as her "darling babies"! What will happen to my garden? Her cats and my cats have been digging up my bulbs...the ones I found on the ground yesterday and the day before.

Came back to find Myfanwy cleaning the cooker and moaning that I am not domesticated enough. Myfanwy got ready to go out. It was her night out with her female friends.

Had tea, watched another debate about Europe and went to bed with a headache.

*Wednesday*

I got up refreshed, ready to go to the golf club to play a round of golf with my former Chief.

When I arrived there it began to pour with rain. We went into the club house and had a drink and lunch until 3-00pm. He informed me that they are all missing me and invited me back on a part-time basis. I might consider it as I am getting bored at home, with Myfanwy's lists and all her training.

I came back home, put the car in the garage and got soaked to the bone while I ran the few steps to the front porch. Got into the house and left a trail of water.

Myfanwy returned early and she barked at me, 'Watch the mess you're leaving behind you! Where have you been? Fresh tea in the pot!'

I replied 'Darling Myfanwy, golfing with the Chief.' But she was no longer listening to me. She was getting ready to go to her yoga class.

I had two cups of tea and a biscuit. All in front of the TV - listened to the latest economic scenarios and fell asleep in the chair. Woke up during another political programme. All repetitive and very boring.

Went upstairs. Myfanwy was gently snoring. Went into my bedroom and closed the door, did not wake her up.

Began reading "War and Peace", recommended by the mother-in-law as a proper retirement novel. Fell asleep again mid first page.

Thursday

Mother-in-law phoned and woke both Myfanwy and me. She wanted to know who to vote for. She informed me in no fancy words that she could not make head or tail about the political predictions regarding Remain or Brexit. She summoned me to go and see her immediately to have breakfast together.

Myfanwy turned over. I showered, got dressed and wrote her a note. I crossed the street and rang the bell 5 successive times and let myself in. Mother-in-law was already at the breakfast table, with toast, homemade apricot preserve, a pot of Assam leaf tea and a bowl of fresh raspberries, blueberries and cherries. She measured me from tip to toe and asked me bluntly, 'If I vote Brexit, will I have English breakfast instead a continental one every morning?' I assured her it had nothing to do with people's meal habits. She also assured me that she rather fancied B. because he was a Latinist and, as she had been a Latin teacher and a headmistress at a private school all her life, she felt they needed to stick together. I learnt that father-in-law, diplomatically, left early for his club, a prim and proper way of referring to his new girlfriend! Mother-in-law is very open-minded about it. The bungalow and the Rolls and the shares are all in her name, so she does not get herself involved with it sentimentally!

I drove into town and had to follow her into every clothes shop and art gallery. I went through the times tables in my head to disguise my irritation.

At the end of three good hours, we stopped for a sushi at the Japanese restaurant opposite the Cathedral. Mother-in-law was in her element with a few measures of sake.

When she'd had enough, I wanted to pay, but she reminded me I was her ally and she insisted on paying the bill.

We got home. Father-in-law was back from his club, had a cup of tea together and then I crossed the road. When I got back home, Myfanwy was just getting up. 'Hurry up! You're late! Change your clothes; we are off to the theatre!' I informed her it was all news to me. She gave me a deep cutting look as she was combing her hair.

I got ready as quickly as I could.

We got to the theatre with one minute to spare before the curtain rose. Don't ask me about the show. I slept through the performance. I felt Myfanwy prodding my ribs from time to time.

At the end, she gave me one of her cutting looks and told me in no chosen words, 'No wonder they retired you! You are a geriatric!' I did not contradict her, because when we first met she was the President of the Debating society at Uni. What an English rose she was!

After the theatre, we went for moussaka at the nearby Greek Restaurant. On the drive home, Myfanwy went on and on about the marathon. Went to bed and fell asleep straightaway.

*Friday*

Got up mid-morning, remembering that our two boys, their wives and the seven grandchildren were due to arrive that very evening. Jack's family who live in Canada were going to stay with us for the weekend and James' lot, who live in New Zealand, was expected at mother-in-law's over the road. Jack was to drive to Scotland on Monday and James was to take his family to Wales. It would be nice to see them and the grandchildren after all this time. Myfanwy questioned me whether I had ordered the food from the supermarket online. I assured her I had done it.

Got the vacuum cleaner out and started from upstairs down. I don't know why we employ a part-time cleaner!

Myfanwy got out of bed and she pointed out I'd had all that time on my hands and could have done this a few days ago, that she cannot have a lie in because of the noise I was making and the dust I was blasting into the rooms!

By 2-00pm I was exhausted. Just then the bell rang and the supermarket delivery van was outside with our order. I sorted them out, as Myfanwy was preparing the beds.

We had a sandwich and a cup of soup. Myfanwy went up and checked the bedrooms. All was in place. We sat in front of the TV. Not sure what was on as I fell asleep again. I got woken up by the arrival of the children. It was past midnight before we all went to bed.

*Saturday*

Got woken up by the screams coming from Myfanwy's bedroom as she was sleeping with the baby to give Jack and Colette, his French-Canadian wife, a break. I went into her bedroom without knocking as it sounded a life and death situation, only to find that it was Myfanwy screaming and not the baby. A spider had stealthily crept in through the open window and landed on the quilt. I picked it up as gracefully as I could, threw it out and closed the triple glazed window quietly. I still think these triple glazed windows were not necessary as the former double glazed ones were brand new! I told Myfanwy 'Darling we are not living in Greenland or in South Georgia or in the Falkland Islands.' 'I have decided' she replied and she arrowed me with one of her theatrical looks. And what Myfanwy wishes is her command...that is if I want a peaceful life!

When we got up properly, I was put in charge of the three grandchildren, because - Myfanwy explained - I have nothing to do anyway and that will enable me to bond with them. After half an hour of bonding, I had cut three of my fingers and I had a plaster on my forehead.

The plan was to go to the zoo, see the animals and have lunch there. Myfanwy would join us later as she had to go to her Zumba class first. Colette, Jack's wife, and Bronwyn, James' kiwi wife, and father-in law offered to join her.

Jack, James, the seven grandchildren, mother-in-law and I went to the zoo. We had lunch and then more animal viewing. All went well, except that mother-in-law's skirt got chewed by a ram from the goat's enclosure. The zoo keepers apologised to her and gave us a lot of vouchers, although the zoo shop was being refurbished.

We got home to an empty house, all very tired with the exception of the grandchildren who were more energetic than expected.

When Myfanwy came back with the daughters-in-law she gave a primordial scream when she entered her bedroom. The walls were all abstract paintings in mascara. 'It's your entire fault, you should have supervised them. Now you'll have to start redecorating on Monday!' There was no sight of father-in-law, who - she informed me candidly - had been dropped at his club!

I got the BBQ ready and mixed some salad. We sat down in the garden and ate. 'You are quiet' Myfanwy said to me.

When we had finished, I was left to clear it all as the grandchildren were put to bed by their parents with an engaging story book.

It took me till midnight to clear up with the help of our two dishwashers. I bypassed the living room, brushed my teeth and went straight to bed.

*Sunday*

Got up, still exhausted from yesterday. My hair was being pulled by Jack's two eldest sons. 'We want to go into the garden', they said, pulling my hands. I got out of bed, wondering about the whereabouts of their parents, gave them some cereals and milk and some juice. 'Mother gives us freshly squeezed orange for breakfast', they told me. So I did exactly that. Then we went into the garden. I let them play as I sat in a recliner and dreamed away.

Myfanwy shook me indelicately and said 'You were supposed to watch the children and play some educational games with them! Look what they did to my roses!' Which I planted and looked after, I thought to myself!

After lunch, we went for a long walk in the gardens of the nearest mediaeval country house with moat and fishpond.

Myfanwy instructed me 'Watch them!' and made for the cafeteria with the daughters-in-law, leaving me with the seven grandchildren. Their fathers went jogging in the grounds, so I was left at their mercy. They chased the ducks, the swans and it's a miracle nobody called the RSPCA.

I managed not to lose any of them!

We had tea in the cafeteria.

Back home, the grandchildren were bathed and settled for the night.

I went into the study and called my Chief and told him I intended to take the part -time job at the station. He informed me that I was in luck because the new superintendent had left on maternity leave on Friday and that they were unable to temporarily replace her. He asked me when I could start. I told him as from tomorrow!

*Monday again*

I was woken by a continuous ringing. I thought my tinnitus was playing me up again. I went to the door. Cousin Mildred was waving a newspaper, which she shuffled under my eyes.

It was open at the For Sale rubric. I went into the kitchen to make a pot of tea; she followed me there and went on,

'I told Cousin Miriam!'' she said in her high-pitched voice. 'Paranoiac, this is how you appear to everybody else! You need to calm down. Nobody is persecuting you.' is what I told her. 'Get real and sort out all this paraphernalia that you've accumulated. It gives your room an air of claustrophobia and that's inadvisable for a detached house ready for sale. Time is of the essence!

I could see she was being difficult. The atmosphere in her house was strange, tense, mainly because she had insisted in buying 20 yards of Parramatta. The friction between her and her paramour, who is a parachutist, started as they were buying this light fabric of wool and cotton to re-upholster their sofas and armchairs. He had insisted on parallel equal stripes, she on plain fabric.

I told her face to face that she needed to re-engage with life. Most of all, to get rid of the paraffin heater which she got from her next-door neighbour, as it's making the central heating redundant. And it's showing our family, who has always been a paragon of excellence in the community, in a bad light to possible buyers. She is short of understanding that selling a house requires delicate and highly skilled manoeuvres when one puts one's home on parade.

It wasn't until the estate agent came to visit the house, pointing out the unnecessary number of cages sheltering multi-coloured parakeets that she broke down in
hysterics. I suggested that she might be living in a parallel universe.

Selling a house – when it's full of wildlife - needed the highest level of order. She came up with lots of excuses and even now, after two good years of exhausting effort, on behalf of all our relatives, friends and several estate agents - who went down with stress - her house is still on the market!

Whose fault is it, I ask myself? She insists on having at least one paravan, some sort of screen with painted parrots in every room! She says it reminds her of her travels as a young girl. Whose fault is it that her paternal grandmother left all that money, which her father spent on trip after trip after trip! And her diet of parboil vegetables, the aroma of which welcomes you as soon as she opens the front door, can only put off any serious buyer. I advocated that the parapet which her man about the house had built from recycled bricks at the front of the house will have to go, as modern houses do not need defence walls like medieval castles did!

Making her understand the reality! I am not sure I have reached a satisfactory conclusion, but one thing I am sure about is she'll find it increasingly difficult to get any viewings of her property, as she is becoming known to all the estate agents in the county as a paranoiac client.'

I drank my tea, and I told Cousin Mildred,

'Look, Mildred, I am due to the station and I must have a shower and get dressed!'

'But…I thought you retired!'

'I did, but I am covering a maternity leave as from today! I must hurry! Help yourself to breakfast and pull the door shut when you leave.'

I sorted myself out and went to the station. It was bliss.

I returned home relaxed. Myfanwy was out. I had a shower, went to bed and fell asleep straightaway.

*Tuesday again*

I am at home as they did not need me at the station today. Myfanwy came earlier than expected and informed me,

'Personal trainer sick! What did you do while I was out?'

'Had elevenses with your mother, per instructed. She was on the phone to her best friend Muriel.'

'I thought they had fallen out, after the church flower rota.'

'They did, but they made up with a phone call.'

'You cut your elevenses short!'

'I had to, as Muriel was due to come to mother-in-law from no. 23 for coffee and a psychological tête-à-tête.'

'Whatever was the matter? Muriel is as tough as a sergeant major!'

'Well, mother-in-law said to me, 'Make yourself scarce, it will all be girls' talk! Nothing that concerns you!'

'Well?' interjected Myfanwy.

'As I reached the door, Muriel was already outside. I let her in. She said to me instead of a greeting, 'Where are you going? I need to sound you out!'

'And?' asked Myfanwy as she fighting with the coffee machine! 'I told you we need to replace it.'

'I'll get onto it pronto.'

'Today, rather than tomorrow!' she snorted.

'Muriel sat herself on mother-in-law's newly reupholstered settee and began to fan herself with mother-in-law's last issue of COUNTRY HOUSES magazine.

She said, 'Peregrine is not himself.' And she burst into tears. Mother-in-law went to the drinks cabinet and – though early in the day – poured Muriel a double whisky.

Muriel drank it in a couple of gulps and resumed the disclosure of Peregrine's problem. 'I was spring cleaning the wardrobes. I did mine, replaced the cedar balls. I thought I

should do the same for Peregrine's wardrobe. I went into his bedroom, I opened the wardrobe door and…' she went sobbing and shaking, situation that forced mother-in-law to present her with another double drink. Muriel drank it straightaway. Mother-in-law and I said nothing, giving her the space to recover and resume her story. 'The wardrobe was bulging with party dresses. As soon as he came from his club after lunch, I confronted him as to the reason of storing those dresses in his wardrobe. He gave me one of his twittering looks direct into my eyes and stuttered, 'I am going to the FESTIVAL, Muriel. Don't try to stop me.'

Muriel went all sobs again. Mother-in-law stepped to the drinks cabinet, but I signalled her a disguised NO. She went to the kitchen to make Muriel a coffee. In the absence of mother-in-law, Muriel turned to me and said, 'What do you think? We have five children together! That's gratitude for all my dedication!'

I did not reply. I looked at the longcase clock adorned with chinoiserie motifs. 'Oh, look at the time. I have to cook lunch. Myfanwy will be back soon from her gym.' At the kitchen door, I said softly 'I am off to cook lunch. Good-bye and thanks.' And I ran to the door and down the drive.'

'Let's not jump the gun; you're always hasty with your assumptions; it's your Stone Age mentality!' uttered Myfanwy taking a sip of decaffeinated coffee from sustainable plantations.

*Wednesday again*

Back from the station, still enthusiastic about seeing my colleagues. All quiet, just paperwork and checking an old murder case in the archives.

Myfanwy and her best friend Consuelo are having tea in the morning room, unaware I am almost napping in the sunset living room, a glass of gin and tonic in hand.

I could hear them clearly.

'Maddie, go and play with Lotte!' I can hear Consuelo encouraging her youngest.

'Don't want to. Don't like her.' Utters the girl assertively.

'You see, Consuelo, what I am struggling with here!' Myfanwy says as she pours some more hot water into the teapot. 'I barely have a minute to myself. It's the Chambers, the clients' cases, the courts...Barely time for my Zumba, Yoga or wrestling nowadays since Dip's retirement! This is what I need now! I keep reminding him of his duties as a husband and as a father of four. He is getting geriatric by the day! How has your week been so far?'

'I know exactly what you mean! Says Consuelo. 'Lots of cases Ilya has been shuffling in my direction. He insisted on me taking the case about that Chef! I declined to represent it as I do not like cooking, that's why we share a cook with my mother.'

'Well, well, well! That's why he came into my office yesterday and begged me on his knees to take the case. No man kneeled in front of me since Dip proposed on our trip to Vietnam as Saigon was falling. I wonder if he thought that was that! Ilya had trouble in getting up...I had to give him a hand onto the armchair.' Says Myfanwy checking her face in the silver teapot. 'It's this client's fault. He did a runner and went to work abroad, after he had been summoned by the Courts for a driving offence! Nobody heard anything from him, his wife and several of his mistresses, all oblivious to one another! Silence! He was declared dead in absentia! After seven years, his wife applied for a death certificate. Meanwhile, he was deported from his adopted country as his passport had expired. He came back, and found his wife had remarried. He wants his house and his land back, though not his remarried wife. He went back to the Courts, but the judge upheld the previous decision. Our Chambers have been appointed to represent him at the Supreme Court! It will be difficult to get to the bottom of it as he appears to have no documents, just affidavits.'

Consuelo smiled with her hazelnut eyes. 'Do you remember how we got stuck on our gap year in Argentina, when the border control told us that our British Passports were not valid in their country and they were very suspicious about us as we kept speaking Welsh?'

'Oh, Consuelo, I remember…how we argued and argued first in English and then in Spanish…and then they let us through as they were closing the flight, the last before the start of the Falkland War… how we hated the food, only beef for breakfast, beef for lunch and beef for dinner, and how we both got into that tango course.'

'We were the best there and the prettiest. Pity the men were bulky and short! We were one head, at least, taller than them, Myfanwy!'

'At least…and they could not pronounce my name.'

'They kept asking me if I was born in Argentina with a name like Consuelo. I did not want to elaborate that when mummy was about to give birth to me she was reading a book about Charles Spencer Churchill, 9th Duke of Marlborough.'

Maddie is back, her hair untidy and covered in chopped leaves. 'What's up Maddie? Where is Lotte?' asks Consuelo.

'In the garden crying.' Answers the girl as she helps herself to a scone from the tray.

'You've got dirty hands!' Utters Consuelo.

'Let her be! Dirty hands keep your antibodies up!'

'Don't tell me how to educate my children, Myfanwy!'

I have no idea what happened next as I fell asleep and woke up after midnight covered in a blanket. Dear Myfanwy thinks of everything!

*Thursday again*

Back from the station. Did some research in the archives on an open murder case, though not as much as I wished; as my work partner brought in photographs of Fran, her younger sister's wedding. The event placed my colleague on the shelf as the eldest in her family. 'Some people have all the luck!' she kept saying bitterly. My colleague put me in the picture about her sister's life story.

"Fran likes to look after herself. She was fresh from her divorce to Francis. It was clever of her to appoint a good law firm to look after her interests. The restored house in Mayfair, the elephant sanctuary, the cellar with champagne top to bottom shelves, the Caribbean private island and the vast villa in Antibes, where Picasso used to paint and is listed in the Catalogue Raisonné are all hers now!

She gets her mirror out her bespoke handbag and admires her plastic surgeon's masterpiece. He made her look early 20ties and not 42!

She has come to the spa to relax. She likes to take a dip in the infinity pool at midday, when no-one is around, though today, she can spy in the waves a pair of perfectly formed dense hairy limbs and jet black curly hair. Her heart begins to flutter like the one of a débutante. He is getting out of the pool. He is perfectly formed, though she can spot webbed feet! It does not matter in the grand scheme of things! Anyway, he would wear socks all day long and one would switch off the light at night-time.

'Hello there! I thought I was alone! I am Hugo by the way!'

'Hi! Call me Fran!'

'Alone? Care for a drink, Fran?'

'Mm…I have been taught not to socialize with strangers, Hugo!'

'You uttered my name…I am no longer a stranger to you, Fran.'

'It is a bit early for me, Hugo!' replies Fran, conscious of her strict daily beauty routine. 'OK, I'll make an exception as we just met!' she says quickly as she might not have another chance.

At the bar, Fran orders an expresso and Hugo orders a Singapore sling.

'Alone at the spa, Fran?'

'Yes, I am, Hugo! Recovering from a divorce! Are you married?'

'Single so far!' and he sips on from his drink.

'Any children, Hugo?' She utters as she plays with her perm.

'No, it would have complicated matters! You see I like horses and horse riding.' Though Hugo does not mention women…not just yet!

'How interesting!'

'What do you like, Fran?'

'I like elephants! I am mad about them since we lived on a tea plantation! That was a long time ago, when I was a little girl and my father managed it.'

'I like elephants too! I went on a trip round the world after I retired from the cavalry. I went to a few elephant sanctuaries. Fascinating, indeed!'

'You look too young to be retired!'

'It's the fresh air and the horses that keep me young! There is nothing more exciting than being in the saddle at a gallop with the air in one's hair!'

Fran touches her forehead. She wishes the air conditioning to be at a lower temperature.

'Do you work, Fran?'

'I used to be a shop assistant. Francis, my ex swept me off my feet age 19. Not had a chance to pass any high school exams. Not that it mattered! He offered me the world. And it was the world! Until he decided otherwise!'

Their eyes locked.

'Your room or mine?' He asked and his deep blue eyes drowned into the abyss of her azure eyes.

It was a rushed wedding and he became husband number 2 out of 7, the father of her only child."

I did not express an opinion and let the day go by. I returned home from the station, relaxed, took my shoes off and made myself a cup of tea, switched on the TV set and fell asleep during the news.

*Friday again*

This morning I got the car out of the garage to go to the station and I saw an ambulance at the top of our street. As I drove, I could see the mangled remains of a car. My mobile began ringing as soon as I arrived at the station. Mother-in-law wanted me at her house as soon as I arrived back from work.

Work day uneventful. Old and new cases, nothing out of the ordinary.

Got home just in time to avoid a downpour. I put the car in the garage, grabbed an umbrella and ran over the road to mother-in-law's. She offered me a stiff drink and a cheese sandwich. In her highly educated accent mother-in-law told me about the incident with the ambulance in our street. It involved a young man called Rick entangled in a love triangle. She got the story from the postman who is a great loss to the secret services.

The rain touched the pavements and drifted away. Rick put the foot on the accelerator. He was eager to reach Juliet's home in good time to read his three kids a story before they went to bed. Juliet insisted on the ritual, though he had always considered it was a woman's duty to nurse her children. After all that was why he had always insisted in

keeping his status clear as a partner and not as a husband to Juliet, who was gradually losing her looks, sinking into fatty layers round the middle and bags under her deep blue eyes…though her boeuf bourguignon was delicious.

Foot on the accelerator, Rick thought as he brushed a chestnut curl from his forehead,

'What a lucky escape! What's the matter with these lasses? He was not going to be a fool! No marriage for him! No way! Better dead than married!'

Which was rather drastic if he came to consider it rationally? He knew what Kate was aiming at and he had been trying to avoid it like the plague. Today, his mobile had been red hot with her calls. He is glad he told her bluntly during her last call,

'It's all over Kate! I don't have the emotional make up to put up with your demands and tantrums' and he gentlemanly switched off his phone.

Rick was also glad he had stood his ground with Gemma. She was his Wednesday girl while her flatmate Kate was working at the village pub.

She made him be late now. Why did she have to call him from work and give him an ultimatum? Threats of killing herself he was immune to! He had already heard it many times from other girl-friends and partners. That was not the way to threaten him!

21

He thought of Gemma and shuddered. 'Marry me or let's part straightaway!' she said to him smirking, when

Kate, Gemma's best friend and house mate showed herself from nowhere at the door of Gemma's bedroom.

Kate was his Monday girl, when Gemma was doing nights at the supermarket.

These young lasses had left him with no choice but save himself from their claws. He put on his pants and his socks inside out with one hand, and grabbed his jacket with the other. Gemma began throwing things at him so that he had to button his shirt and put on his shoes outside the front door. A boy riding a bike went past, burst into laughter and pointed two fingers at him.

Rick rushed down the drive and once inside his car, he put on his tie and his coat, checked himself out, and counted his blessings. He phoned Juliet and let her know he was to be home in twenty minutes.

Rick put the foot on the accelerator.

Upstairs, Gemma's wailing was criss-crossing the thin walls of the Victorian cottage. Downstairs, Vodka glass in hand, Kate looked for the biggest potato in the vegetable tray. She extracted it from the pile. She went to her sewing wooden box. She took out her collection of needles. She sat herself comfortably on the high kitchen chair. She began by scratching two circles on the uneven surface. She contoured a triangle for a nose and two joining lines for a mouth. She smiled a wicked smile and agreed in her mind, 'Oh, yes! I am getting there!' She began unpicking the needles dormant on

their petit point cushion. She carefully placed them, one by one, deep into the potato, inside the contour of the eyes, the nose, the mouth…and last…in the place of the heart…'Oh, yes…'

Rick put the foot on the accelerator…

'Rick, wake up Rick! Yes, open your eyes, Rick! Can you hear me, Rick? Squeeze my hand if you can hear me, Rick!' "

A shiver went down my spine. I hope that the young man recovers. No doubt the postman will keep mother-in-law informed, who will inform me and all her friends and neighbours. No doubt about that. I went back home. All quiet! Myfanwy had left me a note. She was out at her Pilates class. I poured a whisky and began to read "War and Peace" from page one again and I managed three pages.

*Saturday again*

An eventful start of the weekend! First thing in the morning, I took mother-in-law to the hospital for an elective cataract operation. Myfanwy delegated me to accompany her as father-in-law and she are too close to mother-in-law and besides, they feel uncomfortable in hospitals, they say! She insisted that she needed to recharge her batteries during the weekend, and I was the one who chose to retire and I had nothing to do all day long!

Mother-in-law's optician made her a pair of glasses, but the lenses were not right, and to save him remaking them free of charge, as it was his obvious fault, he referred her to the university hospital.
 The specialist at the hospital told her on that very visit that,
'You have a very small cataract. You can have it operated now, in six months or in two years.'
'What do you advise me to do?' Asked mother-in-law.
'Well, you'll have to have it operated at some time in the future, might as well be earlier than later!' he told her as he was shuffling some papers on his desk.
Mother-in-law went home a right mess - as hospitals disturb her deeply - and as she waited for the procedure, she went through all sort of scenarios and came to the conclusion that as Horatio Nelson and Gordon Brown rode into history with one eye, she should be about able to manage from day to day! If all went wrong!
But all went well and we were on our way home.
As I drove, I remembered Myfanwy's emergency shopping list. We stopped at one of our local supermarkets. I cannot explain why a small provincial town needs six supermarkets!
We queued at the deli counter. A mother and two small children, a boy and a girl were in front of us. The boy was pulling his sister's hair, kicking their shopping trolley and making loud noises. Shoppers ignored them.

'Stop pushing the trolley! Have a bit of patience!' the young mother admonished the little boy, who turned towards us, the next in the queue, and was stunned. His eyes measured mother-in-law. He turned towards his mother, but could not make any eye contact with her. He turned once again towards mother-in-law to be certain. He stared at her left eye, the one covered by a transparent eye-patch secured by three strips of micropore tape and he went very quiet.

At the till, I checked Myfanwy's emergency shopping list once again.

I delivered mother-in-law home. Her agency nurse was already there to look after her for the duration of the weekend, as father-in-law had a golf tournament to go to as a spectator.

I sorted the shopping and I made myself a coffee - I like to grind my own beans - Myfanwy has left me a note. She had gone out with her colleagues because they had tickets to the Opera.

I sigh with relief. The house is all mine.

*Bank Holiday Monday*

I got up at lunchtime and I went down to Myfanwy's bespoke kitchen in my pyjama bottoms. If she could see me this very moment!

I made myself a cappuccino and a slice of brioche with apricot jam. I fancy some scones for the afternoon. I could take some to mother-in-law's who has got her cousin Tamsin with her new French husband who live in York, visiting for the weekend. It reminds me of Mafalda, our eldest. She went to uni. first, to find a partner, and second, to acquire some learning!

It's so random how events string themselves! In her case, her bespoke Fang Shui scones were her making.

According to Mafalda, it all went like this,

'I think we've met before' the young man who had tried to catch young Mafalda's eye during her train journey from Norwich to London whispered in her ear.

Mafalda stopped and looked at him and it all came back to her. That very moment! He had been her great unknown. She was about to start her first year at uni. Myfanwy, aware of her

24

anxiety, enrolled her in a cookery course. Mafalda went to the community centre to begin her course one early summer evening. As she was late as usual, she opened the first door in immediate view. The room was packed with women. She said to herself that must be good.

'You're late!' She heard a male voice stutter in her ear.

'I am here for the cookery class!' muttered Mafalda ill at ease. She had a distorted view to the front of the room. A male model with blonde curls displayed all his whimsical parts. Pirouetting pressure swiped inside young Mafalda. Her breathing levitated for moments. She closed her eyes and hissed like a bursting balloon on the Bastille Day, 'I am in the wrong class!' and she retreated, her face of a beetroot colour.

She found her Back to Basics cookery class and spent two uneventful hours there, followed by two weeks of intensive cooking and baking. She was the less gifted in her group, what the present PM would class as 'steady, strong and stable'.

During the break, she got to meet Al, the owner of that rebel voice and they let off some steam together, mainly in her uncle's garlic meadow, which he kept on display for the inspectors of the agricultural ministry, in case they visited and plotted to cut his EU subsidies. On August afternoons, as the west wind ruffled the crop of garlic, she offered him her first scone made all on her own.

'You could make a good living of that kind of thing, if you follow the Feng Shui laws' he said as he took – uninvited - a second scone from her box.

In September, Al and Mafalda parted as good friends and promised, with tears in their eyes – mainly in his eyes – to keep in touch with daily e-mails.

Studying English and swamped in essays, Mafalda did not reply to Al's elaborate crafted words.

Every evening, back from her lectures and research in the library, not on any English authors, but into Feng Shui, she began baking scones on a grand scale. First she offered them to her friends and then she took them to the uni. coffee shop in the hope of an order. The manageress took a bite and ordered six dozens for the following day. A week on, she ordered one hundred scones.

Mafalda's weather vane changed direction. She went to the local supermarket and one bite on, the manager gave her a trial order.

What followed next was extensively recorded in advertisements made by Mafalda's best friend Jacob, the owner of Copernicus, a sensitive Yorkshire terrier. Mafalda's chain of bespoke bakeries is open for business every day, at home and overseas, and the Japanese especially cannot have enough of her Feng Shui scones!

I made the scones and went to mother-in-law for afternoon tea. Cousin Tamsin who is working on the family tree was visiting. She got stuck in the reign of James I. She spread the family tree on the floor from one wing of the house to the other. She told us enthusiastically,

'I cannot wait. I am so looking forward to visit the Old Museum of Curiosities in Oldwitch. We'll drive there first thing tomorrow.'

'But Tamsin, it's the Bank Holiday! The traffic is madness! ... with your lack of proper motorways!'

'Pierre, stop thinking continental! It's history alive here! Submerge yourself in it! This hamlet is the oldest inhabited place in the country that can trace its roots, with documents, as direct descendants of William the Curious. This is how they appear on the Jute Tapestry, embroidered by Elisa the nun, one of the female ancestors of our own family.

Pierre, I wish to visit this place to see the small version of this tapestry, known in the history of art as the Oldwitch Tapestry, size 59"x74" - now with cotton cream backing - woven in dyed jute in the Jacquard style.

Another branch of the family still owns everything around as Seigneurs of the Land. They all live in the only fortress hamlet of the land mentioned in François' Book, the non-illuminated version at page 13.

Pierre, do you realise, we are practically related to them?

I read online that the hamlet is known for its high quality jute. Last year, the jute producers had a close encounter with the tax inspectors, regarding the way they register their revenues, situation that led to nothing, as it came to light, after six months of investigation, that the hamlet is, according to old tax documents, tax exempt!

The tapestry is said to have miraculous qualities. Pilgrims from all over the world visit the hamlet, and upon paying £250 per head, per night, they can get a room outside the walled hamlet, with no bathroom, and WC at the back of the park. They may enter the hamlet during the day only, and touch the tassel trimmed tapestry. This is famed for bringing a positive change in one's circumstances!

And there is the unexplained!

Every five years, for 24 hours only, the oldest female in the hamlet falls into a deep trance after the Midsummer's Feast, and the tapestry begins to smell of fresh wild garlic. When the oldest female in the hamlet recovers, she forecasts events that will happen in the following five years. Like Stalin's five year plans!

This year, after a succession of deaths from her rivals, the oldest lady in the hamlet is Lady Oldwitch.

Pierre, tomorrow will be my turn to enter the chamber to see the display, and be able to identify the pattern described in the £5 literature on sale at the museum shop.

What am I going to see? Will I decipher its secret?'

I left Cousin Tamsin, Pierre and mother-in-law debate and I returned home to an improving session of crosswords. And with nothing else to do I went to bed early.

*Friday, 13th*

An uneventful week. At last I can have some peace and quiet.

Myfanwy has left for a short curling weekend. I did the washing up per instructed - dishwasher and hand finish afterwards - I drove the three miles to the stables to check on Myfanwy's five rescued donkeys. Last week, I offered to take them to a donkeys' sanctuary with a good dowry donation, but she had none of it. She acidly told me, 'You don't understand human nature, I connect with them!'.

I am counting the days until Tuesday and Thursday, my part-time work at our station. I went back fulltime after retirement for Vicky's maternity leave. She left it so late that she was delivered of a healthy baby girl that very night. One month on and she's back - she read her husband his rights and he had to take a sabbatical from his bank so he is now a house husband. The chief could give me two days only. It's a break for me from daily elevenses with mother-in-law.

This morning, she told me of our youngest tribulations. I quote their conversation,

'Grandma, I am devastated. He chose to settle for the twins.'

'Who? What twins?' Mother-in-law asked Genevieve.

'The Italian accordion player, the one entangled with the twin girls. You know! You were there! At Donnafugata, you were there in October last.' The lass said and began to sob.

'You have not been introduced, and you have never seen him before and after.'

'But I love him grandma. I would go to the end of the world for him!' Was Genevieve's reply.

'And what would you have done with him?'

'Madly love him, you would not understand grandma.'

'What about Freddie? He seems keen on you? You go swimming and skiing together?'

'Ha-ha! He plays the harp, grandma! We are strictly best friends!'

Mother-in-law replied in her wisdom,

'Look at grandpa and I, a very successful marriage, 50 years of bliss.'

'Yes?' replied my distressed daughter. 'Where is he now…he is always at his club…when are you together?'

Mother-in-law looked at the inexperienced lass and replied,

'You need to take a leaf from your mother's book! And mine! Learn from her control. Her boarding school education, Swiss finishing schooling and Oxbridge made her the controlled person she is nowadays.'

'Grandma, I dream of a relationship based on love!'

'You dream, your dream, all delusion! In our family, women married for money and power, love fades away like melting ice. It shines; it reflects and then melts away.'

'But grandma, that makes you and mother a geisha!'

'Beware of appearances! Fragile on the outside and steel inside!'

Mother-in-law asked me to have a serious discussion as father to daughter. I have nothing to say to the lass. She can do whatever she wishes. It's not for me to tell her what to do.

Nowadays lasses are the power generation, we lads are in the background, continuously scrutinised for any mistake.

I remember that very trip from a different angle!

The bell rings. At this hour? I turn to check the alarm clock. It's midmorning. We got back from the airport at 2.00 past midnight and I feel a chill is digging deep into my bones. From 30 degrees C to -2 degrees C! That's what you get! I open the bedroom window and call out, 'I'll be down in a minute'.

I descend in my pyjamas and open the door. The storm hisses and torments the trees. There is no-one there. On the step I see my box of arancini. I must have dropped it last night as I entered. I am glad Myfanwy is still asleep. She would have shouted 'Clumsy man!' And other endearing observations! From her dictionary of sarcastic remarks!

I pick up the box, close the door and enter the kitchen. I open the box and I take the arancini out, one by one, place them in a plastic box and then into the fridge. I cannot help but keep one for now and I begin to grind coffee for one.

I take a bite from my arancini and pour water into the coffee machine. How time flies. Yesterday we were driving along the steep and bendy roads leading to Donnafugata. It was All Saints Day and the cemeteries were full of vehicles, hordes of people and the traffic police. I take a sip of coffee. It was a good holiday, in spite of Myfanwy bossing me day in and day out. After a life spent together, one becomes oblivious to one's other half's obvious faults. So clear to everyone else from day one!

As we got off the plane at Palermo airport, Myfanwy said to me,

'I shall drive. You got concussed on the landing. You should not have allowed that young man drop his bag on your head! You should watch what you do in the future.'
'But Myfanwy, it was an accident. He was not aware!'
'These foreigners!' blasts Myfanwy unsympathetically. 'Incorrect, Myfanwy! We are the foreigners, in their own country!'

'We are the ones with the money, the investment, the banks and the Brexit!' she shouts.
'I can hear you loud and clear, Myfanwy!
'Well, what side am I voting for?' Butts in mother-in-law,

buttoning her loud crimson cardigan. 'Not at the moment, we're on holiday, mummy! You are tired after the flight. We'll be in our hotel in no time!' I place mother-in-law at the back seat of the car, next to our youngest, so far, unmarried, daughter. Then I shuffle all our bags in the boot of the rented 4X4.                                                    I am about to get into the car on the driver's side. 'Oh no! You cannot drive on the right. Could get distracted with all your daydreaming and we'll end in a ditch!' stresses Myfanwy.

The drive to Donnafugata happens amongst ancient olive groves, the branches empty of olives and goats munching diligently by the side of the bendy roads. The olive harvest is in full swing, small and big, young and old, nets under the ancient trees and reels of sweat.

Today, the soil is parched and the noon sun is a frying pan. A few goats are nibbling at the thorny bushes.

Myfanwy parks the car at Donnafugata Palace.

We follow the white path. On both sides two story buildings rise bleached from the Southern sun, and lifeless dogs are displayed in the path.

'Are they dead?' I ask for the sake of it. 'They are having a siesta!' Myfanwy replies in her sarcastic tone. As we walk on to Donnafugata Palace, I fan myself with the Panama hat I borrowed from father-in-law, who has remained at home busy at his Club.

We enter the massive gates of the palace. At the ticket office we are told the palace is closed for lunch.

We retrace our steps and enter the only eatery there, a trattoria. The young daughter of the owner sits us at a table and brings the menu. We order lamb, beef and rabbit with house potatoes and Sicilian vegetables. The two huge dining rooms fill in with no table to spare. Drinks are brought in followed by steaming food. Gargantuesque portions. The most delicious barbequed lamb I have ever eaten. As we are eating, I hear accordion music coming from the other side of the dining room. My daughter stops eating and stares mesmerised. I turn and I notice a young man, with raven curly hair. He is playing Sicilian tunes of deep longing. He is playing of the dust of the land, the precarious life of his people, the Sicilian cuore, and the depth of the soul.

'That's the one, mother!' Unreserved, she blurts out.

'Steady on, you don't know him!'

The waitress brushes by our table. Our youngest daughter pulls her by one arm and Myfanwy by the other.

'Signorina, dimmi per favore/ tell me please. Who is that divine accordion player?' asks Myfanwy as our youngest daughter airs her mouth.

'It's my cousin, Signora.' She says as she is about to leave.

'Is he betrothed' carries on my uninhibited youngest daughter.

'You see the twins? Next to him?'

'The pregnant ones?'

'The very ones? He got both of them pregnant. It was an accident, a misunderstanding!' The young waitress comes closer, her words a whisper, 'They took a bet! He did not know there were two of them! They played a trick on him. As he was courting one of them, they both decided to get pregnant by him. He did not know who was who. Now he pours all his soul into the music. The twins' father had a word with him. Afterwards, the culprit spent a month in the intensive care ward of the orthopaedic department in the hospital in Palermo.'

'What's going to happen now?'

'Nothing, as long as both of them stick to him. As long as this happens, their father will do nothing as the twins are the apple of his eye.'

'Pity, the man has potential as a son-in-law!' concludes Myfanwy. Big tears shine on the face of our youngest daughter.

'Another candidate gone!'

'What with Brexit! He does not even wear a suit!' buts in mother-in-law and she takes another bite from her rabbit stew!

I cross the road and come home. I cannot wait for the peace and quiet of our station. To handle our suspects. To stay away from all these psychological issues! I'll make myself a cup of Horlicks and pass the time watching some TV. I hope it's not reality TV!

*Saturday, 14th*

The phone wakes me up. I ignore it from under the quilt. It goes on and on. I want to switch it off, but it's mother-in-law again!

'Come at once. I could have lost my life last night.'

It must be serious. I shower and get dressed as fast as in my training days, I cross the road and I let myself in.

'Help yourself to breakfast' she says. 'I had the most disturbing experience last night! Sylvia gave me a lift to the outskirts of Old witch where both of us attend our monthly reading session.'

…and she begins,

'Mind the stones' Sylvia advises me as we are getting out of our friend's remote cottage, after a spot of reading, lots of wine and gossip. It's almost midnight and I get into her car. Light has long surrendered and deep darkness filters into every nook and cranny.

'It's late and I don't like to drive in the dark.' My fellow reader goes on.

'Right you are, after all that information and doom prediction by old Lady Oldwitch. I reply not too sure of myself, as a passenger who had had a remote brush with driving and thirteen unsuccessful driving tests!

'Nonsense' utters my driver sure of herself.

We get into her car, she starts the engine and there we go down the slope, and past our friend's gates, and into the pitch-dark road. There are no street lamps. It is pitch-black past the hedgerows.

'I cannot find the lights switch. Only if I had a torch!' I hear her utter.

'Then stop the car!' I find myself reply in a whisper.

'…only if I could find the lights switch! …only if I had a torch!' She is now hyperventilating. The darkness clings to the shape of her face.

'Stop the car!' I hear myself shout in her direction. Can I smell the scent of fear or is it the mist?

It must be midnight now. There is no car in the narrow one-vehicle road. A feeble moonlight hovers over phantom brambles. All is still except for Sylvia's car. I can guess my driver fumbles with the commands on the dash board.

'I don't know what to do! Only if I had a torch!' I can detect tears. Sight and sense elude both of us.

'Just take the foot off the accelerator and apply the breaks' I hear myself order her.

I have butterflies in my stomach and all other sort of insects whose names I don't know zoologically. I sense Sylvia lower the window and feel the flutter of wings or is it a panic attack or environmental hysteria?

It's all his fault! Your father-in-law's. He went to his club telling me with a smile 'You'll enjoy your reading session amongst your friends from THE LADIES' BOUDOIR!'

The car comes to an abrupt stop, still in the road and not on the deep side ditch along the country lane.

My driver keeps trying the dashboard and EUREKA, the lights come on and she utters with a sigh of relief:

'It's OK now. Nothing to worry about! I know what I am doing!'

I get home in one piece and I find your father-in-law back from his club and fast asleep, snoring in the rhythm of the TV set.

I advised mother-in-law to order a taxi in the future.

*Sunday, 15th*

Myfanwy and I went to mother-in-law for Sunday lunch. After two neat gins, mother-in-law was in her element, reminiscing about Genevieve, her favourite grandchild, what happened when we moved house, and what Genevieve discovered in the wardrobe.

Most adults believe that Genevieve is a mischievous little girl, as they do not know the secrets of an inquisitive young girl in the making. Nosy as nature has made her, she wants to learn everything about her new home where the family moved at the beginning of last month.

She had combed the ground floor and now she is into the first floor. Knee socks at the ankle, fresh stains on her bespoke blue dress from the raspberry bushes and hair ribbon at an angle, she is checking the pieces of furniture the previous owners had left behind.

She is attracted by a grand and ornate triple door mahogany wardrobe. She had planned to tackle it the previous day, just when grandmamma called her for luncheon. In their family, she is referred to by 'that nosy and feisty child', who likes to annoy her sister and her brothers, who are admittedly two ugly looking specimens, lacking the bespoke personality of their female siblings.

Unintimidated and super eager, Genevieve is face to face with the wardrobe. She checks its three doors. They are locked. No problem, mechanically inclined, Genevieve has a skeleton key that she had procured from her cousin Elgin, who is a very greedy boy. He had stolen the key from the gardener and sold it to Genevieve for a small bag of pistachio nuts.

In goes the key.

In the kitchen, grandmamma is supervising the cherry preserves. Their part-time kitchen maid is a clumsy young lass who is still in training and unaccomplished after a year.

'Ah!' A deep piercing scream, the level of the decibels of a cannon blast, shakes the Victorian kitchen, disturbs the alignment of the jars on the oak table and rattles the open windows. The sky goes a lead colour as the park ravens nesting in the oak trees take off.

'What is happening?' asks grandmamma assertively. The part-time kitchen maid drops the jar with cherry preserve all over the kitchen floor, and burst into tears.

'Genevieve! Where are you? I said and I say it again, the sooner she goes to boarding school, the better for everyone!'

The scream intensifies and grandmamma and kitchen maid are going up the grand stairway, two steps at a time. There they bump into the part-time gardener, muddy boots and a geranium flowerpot in hand.

The three of them reach the open door from where the decibels keep erupting.

'There you are, Genevieve. Stop screaming and pull your socks up!' Grandmamma checks Genevieve's appearance and finds her intact.

Genevieve's screaming is making the Murano chandelier rotate anticlockwise. The young girl is pointing to the wardrobe.

'How did you manage to open the door?'

Genevieve is gasping and points to the door of the wardrobe which is ajar.

Grandmamma opens it widely. Several corpses, in various degrees of decay, slide from the bowls of the furniture on the well-polished oak boards.

Next door neighbour, Mrs Gregson, the newly retired commissioner's mother-in-law, is having elevenses with Mrs Barnard, one of her best friends for the time being.

'What's going on with your new neighbours? It sounds like a matter of life and death!' utters Mrs Gregson and both ladies rush to find out what they can. They open the wrought iron gate and run up the path towards the front door. They do not bother to ring the bell as the front door is wide open. Like hounds, they follow the screams and climb up the stairs.

They enter the room. A little girl is screaming with her eyes shut, an elderly woman is howling red face like an erupting volcano, a young lass is shedding tears the size of freshly harvested peas. A middle aged man covered in mud looks stunned and is squashing the geraniums in a flower pot tight to his chest.

Mrs Gregson, who has been blessed with full comprehensive initiative, takes a look and identifies the cause of the distress as originating from inside the wardrobe.

'Oh, here they are! My son-in-law, the former commissioner and his team had been looking for them for some good years now. Unsolved, the case is still open. It made the front page of all the broad sheets and the tabloids at the time. A whole family wiped out, except a three year old son who kept repeating the word <sardines> and had a key round his neck. Nobody paid any attention to him as he was there just for the weekend.

We returned home and Myfanwy told me off because - she said – I encouraged her mother to go on and on and that now she has a throbbing headache and that she needs to have an urgent rest in her bedroom with the shutters closed.

It's TV for me again and a cup of tea!

*Monday, washing day*

I do not follow any of these old customs. I do not do any washing on Mondays. Mother-in-law summoned me to her elevenses. She wanted to explain to me why she was not speaking to either Mrs Gregson, her childhood friend, or to Mrs Barnard for the time being, who have become gossip masters! This hush-hush conversation has reached mother-in-law's sensitive ears!

'Mrs Gregson, I shall have that second cup of coffee after all. Tell me more! What's going on at Myfanwy's? Haven't seen her for ages.'

'Have a bit of patience! I'll come to that! She came to visit me last Saturday, a week tomorrow, to ask me to look after her cats. She told me they were going to Wales. She appealed to my discretion as to the purpose of her visit. I reassured her that it will all remain closed between these four walls.'

'Mrs Gregson, I understand, a promise is a promise.'

''Have a bit of patience! I'll come to that! My dear, I can make an exception. How long have we known each other?'

'Mrs Gregson, since I went to London to the Klimt exhibition. We met in the tearoom, as the restaurant was being refurbished.'

''Have a bit of patience! I'll come to that! True, true. You've got a good memory.'

'So they all tell me!'

''Have a bit of patience! I'll come to that! They left for Wales as she got an inheritance.'

'Mrs Gregson, who from? Not that I need to know!'

'Have a bit of patience! I'll come to that! They went to Wales in his new Porsche car, the one he bought on e-bay after a night of drinking!'

'Yes, Mrs Gregson, I know, you have already told me!'

''Have a bit of patience! I'll come to that! I don't know if you recall. There must have been about ten years ago. Or there could have been fifteen…'

'The Jubilee!'

'Have a bit of patience! I'll come to that! Her uncle Robert, or Bob as they called him came from Wales. He was all Tweeds and golf. She brought him here for tea once. Introduced him as the fifth Baronet!'

'You must have got your Rose china out! Did you make a Victoria cake?'

'Have a bit of patience! I'll come to that! Not a Victoria sponge, but a Madeira cake, my daughter made at home economics classes the day before. Myfanwy took me unprepared. Though she apologised. He came out of the blue in an Aston Martin. It got all the neighbourhood children in a right frenzy.'

'It must have been a shock to them, they must have built the new extension much later!'

'Have a bit of patience! I'll come to that! They had only two bedrooms then, one for them and their old tomcat and one for their children.

'The cat that passed away last summer!'

''Have a bit of patience! I'll come to that! Indeed! The very same one! Fur all over the bed and the carpet! Not to mention the upholstery! Their guest had to go B&B overnight as he was allergic to cats!'

'Just like my youngest!'

'Have a bit of patience! I'll come to that! Apparently he went to Japan and attempted to climb Mount Fuji, one of his dreams, and was killed in an avalanche. They found him after six months, at the foot of the mountain, when the snows melted. A terrible end for a man of means!'

'And a Baronet!'

'Have a bit of patience! I'll come to that! He left Myfanwy's family – wait for it - his castle in Wales – newly re-wired, re-plumbed, with underfloor heating. A large deer park, two villages and six working farms, as well as some money and some shares.'

'What about the title?'

'Have a bit of patience! I'll come to that! All, with the condition they look after his collection.'

'What kind of collection, Mrs Gregson?'

'Have a bit of patience! I'll come to that! That's the whole issue! The collection! On their first visit to view the inheritance, Myfanwy almost had a fit. The castle main reception room was a reptile house the butler kept under lock and key. The snakes were – according to the Baronet – left free to explore the space.'

'What will she do now?'

'Have a bit of patience! I'll come to that! The inheritance is all linked to the snake collection. No snake collection, goodbye inheritance! It will all go to the RSPCA!'

'Oh, dear, Mrs Gregson!'

'Have a bit of patience! I'll come to that! Now the butler has given his notice. He was left only with a maid and a cleaner who are his daughters. All the other staff was agency and they usually stayed one week max.!'

'Well, with Myfanwy's present expensive standards, she cannot give it up!'

'Have a bit of patience! I'll come to that! Certainly not, she is very resilient. She has already contacted an anxiety coach. She hopes to overcome her reptile phobia.'

'Has she got a deadline?'

'Have a bit of patience! I'll come to that! They have nine months to sort it out.'

'What if she falls pregnant again?'

''Have a bit of patience! I'll come to that! That will not happen. He had the operation after he bought the Porsche! She insisted! Four was her limit! Another cup of coffee?'

'Thank you, Mrs Gregson, two is my limit! Oh, look at the time. I must be off.'

I remember the episode with the Porsche that has always been a sensitive issue between Myfanwy and I. It happened as it happened!

'Where are you?'

'Hi, Griff! Sorry I couldn't make our golf session.'

'Where are you, Dip? It was a disaster. With the Captain ill and all that!'

'Well, if I were to tell you about all my troubles and tribulations!'

'What are you on about?'

'I'm with Myfanwy on our way to Norwich!'

'To Norwich? Are you having me on?'

'No, Griff, not on this occasion!'

'TICKETS, PLEASE!'

'Hang on a minute, Griff! You see, Myfanwy and I are on the way to Norwich! Last night, we went to Selwyn's stag night!'

'I was there, don't you remember, Dip?'

'Anyway, to cut a long story short, I got home worse for wear. Irresistible Myfanwy went on one of her rages, called me irresponsible and locked the bedroom door. I went into the

living-room and I went on eBay! You know how I am on eBay!'
'Addicted more likely, Dip! Are you joking? Everybody knows!'
'Myfanwy wanted to look for a new house in the city…'
'Did you find something you both like?'
'Wait a minute! I went on eBay and I began to bid.'
'What for, Dip?'
'You know how much I wanted to get a white Porsche?'
'Since we were at nursery, you kept showing everybody your white Porsche toy car!'
By now there is dead silence in the compartment and fellow travellers are all ears. The ticket collector has forgotten to move on to check the tickets.
'I kept bidding and bidding! I was in a frenzy, not too aware of all that!'
'You don't say! You must have been way over the limit! You need to take us for a spin!'
'In the morning, I felt a strong kick and my ears swarmed with expletives from Myfanwy who was very strung up! I tried to get my bearing! She kept calling me irresponsible. And other colourful words, I cannot repeat them now! You know how she is when she gets worked up! She pushed a beaker full of coffee under my nose and I gradually drank it. My head felt like a punch bag!'
'And…and…'
'You used my laptop to bid on eBay!' she uttered in a very high-pitched voice that committed virtual surgery through my brain! 'What are you talking about?' I uttered softly. 'Look, you bought a white Porsche! Look at the price! What's the matter with you?' She went all red in the face! What are you talking about? I uttered gently. She showed me the communication. 'We don't need another car! Forgot? You lost your driving licence last Christmas and I am the one who drives you around! Remember that?' It's not far! It's at a stone's throw away! Is this what you think?' she said! Look! You should see how she is spearing me with her steel eyes now! 'It's in Northwich in Cheshire!' I replied as the pressure in my head was intensifying exponentially! 'You must collect

it from Norwich! Not Northwich!' Where is it? 'According to my Google Map, it's in Norfolk, somewhere near London!'

'I see, Dip, you're in deep trouble!'

'Well, indeed! We had to catch the Cardiff to London train, and then had to change in London for Norwich with a few minutes to spare! It cost us a fortune as we did not pre-book! And worst of all, Myfanwy insisted in buying sandwiches at the station. I replied it was not necessary! We'll buy some on the train! I said. Guess what?'

'What? What?'

'To make matters worse there is no buffet car and we are due to arrive in Norwich at 9-35pm and I bet all outlets will be closed at the station. Myfanwy hasn't had any eye contact with me since we left the house. We must spend the night in a hotel now! More expenditure! We'll collect the car in the morning!'

'I bet you cannot wait, Dip!'

'Well, in a way, though Myfanwy has forbidden me to use the word bid!'

'Let's hope you do not break down on the way back!' utters the ticket collector as he resumes his duties.

I had to take my driving licence test again. And I had to suffer the consequences in my career! I try not to think of it!

*Tuesday, ironing day*

The mobile wakes me up. 'Come at once for breakfast! Have you heard?'

Bewildered, I look at time. It's 6.00am.

It takes me over half an hour to get ready. I ignore the telephone as it's mother-in-law again.

At 7.00am I let myself in over the road.

She is straight into the topic,

'I have just read it online and I remain completely puzzled!' she says, hands knotted on her immaculate Tweed skirt. '100 pupils, it was reported.'

'So many? What are you referring to, mother-in-law?'

'Are you listening?! All school girls!'

'Were they on their own!'

'Negative! They had come in for the morning assembly.'

'Their teachers must have been present!'

'They were…they were…The music teacher began the first hymn on the piano!'

'It sounds like a normal school day to me!'

'It would have been…but the girls started to faint, some displayed muscular convulsions and others went into a seizure! I am sure that was what was said, but maybe I was wrong!'

'We'll soon find out! Let's go on line and check the facts!'

Mother-in-law activates her laptop and checks the day's News.

'You're correct! One hundred school girls from a little town in the mountains of Peru were taken to the local hospital. The doctors there observed how they gradually woke up from what looked like a trance. The doctors could not find anything physically wrong with the girls. When questioned by the doctors, all reported experiencing the vision of a ghost with hollow eyes!'

'Mass hysteria! I reply burning myself with the tea!'

'Well you might say that, but the doctors at the hospital could not find any rational explanation! See how it goes on… that a parapsychologist is of the opinion that the young lasses are young and vulnerable in their beliefs and easily impressed by the stories that there had been many victims of terrorism buried in that area. When the soil was excavated to build their school, they found lots of dead bodies, mostly decomposed. The locals believe that the girls went into a trance to communicate with the dead!'

'Who would have thought just one idea put into young minds would have caused such an outcome.' I reply disinterested.

'Don't forget, that many folk from the high mountains of Peru believe in a magical reality!'

'It's the altitude, mother-in-law!'

I yawn and I return home to collect my lunch. The traffic is light today and I manage to reach the station in time.

*Wednesday, cleaning house day*

I do not do any of it, just in emergencies as Myfanwy insists on a part-time cleaner. She considers my effort sub-standard!

I got an e-mail from Genevieve today. She went to teach English in China to forget her Sicilian accordion player.

'For me, Mao's poetry is everywhere! She told me in a chirpy voice.

'It's great to teach in China. I ended up in a middle school, in a remote place of eleven million people, continuously bitten by thick sands incessantly floating from the Gobi desert. You might find it exotic, but not if you were here. Perhaps from a distance, but not if you have to inhale it day in and day out! One day, after the break, I went to the class I was about to teach. I found the door locked and no pupils! I went back to the office and a good 10 minutes into the 40 minutes lesson. I found out from the office staff, in sign language of course, that my class had been relocated to a different classroom on another level.

Bad planning! They are supposed to lead the world!

It's just a dream! It's different here on the ground! Things are not quite as they are portrayed to be! I blame Mao, and my infatuation with his plum blossom poetry. It blinded me! When I read it, it makes me dream!

I went, avoiding the spitting on the floor that did not quite get into the spittoons, to the newly allocated classroom and learnt from my students that only one of them had been told of the location change. I did not know that all is then left to word of mouth! There, I barely settled my 55 pupils when a team of builders opened the door, budged into the classroom and began to loudly bang and take down the windows.

It sounds surreal! From the most up and coming nation in the world!

Apparently, they are totally bankrupt at local level, though they are solvent at government level. The builders got on with their job, ignoring the pupils and me. I looked at the pupils, they looked at me and one of them explained it was common practice that all the building jobs had to be done within school hours. By then, with my questions and the pupils' replies the lesson was gone.

The pupils' reaction? They acted as if it were normal. It's something that can reoccur many times during the school year! The parents say nothing to something like this. It's considered normal! They just keep themselves to themselves and wait for orders from Beijing.

Frustrating on the ground?

One gets used to it! I put it down to the fact that everything here starts and ends with Mao's poetry!'

I smiled. We are all missing her and hope she'll settle into a teaching career.

I'll make myself dinner for one as Myfanwy is going to be late tonight due to her busy work at the Chambers.

Our Genevieve has done well with her teaching. She is now well viewed and respected by her colleagues, parents and pupils. She is assertive just like her mother.

She called me before the GCSE results as she had doubts regarding the success of some of her pupils. Alas Myfanwy could not give her some words of encouragement as she is away most weekends with her hobbies and leisure activities.

This is an example of what goes on in her lessons.

'Good morning class. Ready to begin?'

'Not yet Miss. Callum is crying.'

Miss draws a line on the board and a bubble with Callum's name in it.

'What's the matter, Callum?'

'Miss, Callum came into the classroom upset and with a bit of a headache.'

'Why, Callum? Jenny let him speak for himself.'

'Miss, he is too upset to speak.' And Jenny points to her table mate, who is hiding his head in his folded hands.

'What has happened? Let us see.'

'Miss, Jordan pushed Lucas' so Miss draws another line with a bubble with Lucas' name in it.

'Then Lucas pushed Callum into the wall.' Miss draws a bubble with Lucas' name and a line towards a wall with bricks and a bubble with Callum's name in it.

'But it was not Lucas' fault.'

'Whose fault was it, then?'

'It was Sabrina's, Miss, because she caught the lurgy from some girls in upper school and because she did not want to catch it, she passed it on, Miss! To Lucas, Miss!'

Miss draws another bubble with Sabrina's name and a line towards Sabrina's bubble.

'Then it's all sorted out! Alright, Callum now?'

'Yes, Miss. I am OK, as long as the lurgy is on the board!' and a calm Callum wipes his nose with the sleeve of his jumper.

That's the new generation. I hope her pupils have got at least a PASS, though with the new way of grading the all written exam, it might be tricky, but we must remain hopeful.

*Friday, gardening day*

Mother-in-law invited Myfanwy and I to have dinner together tonight. We went over the road and Myfanwy, after embraces and kisses told us she was unable to stay as the owner of the Chambers has invited all the lawyers and clerks to his country house for the weekend as it was his wife's birthday. Spouses not invited. After Myfanwy left, mother-in-law poured a double whisky for me and a triple for herself. She became animated and began reminiscing about the times of her youth, the first time when her parents took her to a bonfire night à l'anglaise in a little town in Alsace where her parents had inherited a summer cottage. As she recalled, the town was quiet. There was no light at the windows of the houses. The flowers along the riverfront were dying. The pavement cafes were long closed.

Intense buzzing was coming from the Chateau, renovated by its new English owners, Mr & Mrs Candlebody the previous summer.

Adèle - mother-in-law's first name - feared the dark. Her parents had to promise her a list of gifts to persuade her to join them at The Candlebody's party for she did not get on with their children. She disliked them intensely.

When they arrived at the Chateau, at midnight, wide-eyed, she measured the yard with the pile of wood up to the portcullis. She felt breathless with all her five years old.

When the invited crowed – the very good spilled from the capital and the very best the department could offer - lit the fire, Adèle let out one of those rare primordial screams that one hears in horror films or when animals are ritually slaughtered. She was louder than the burning wood on the bonfire. The windows of the Chateau shuddered becoming pixels in the shimmering wind. A shame as they had the original glass and had survived the fury of the French Revolution!

The leaves on the trees shivered in the wind and fell. The wild storm began to torment the ancient oaks in the arboretum, disturbing the sleep of the resident ravens.

I shuddered and felt a chill in mother-in-law's bespoke living-room. She told me laughing, 'It's time for another drink' and she poured me another double whisky and another triple for herself. Peregrine is at his club and he might stay overnight. I'll tell you about my musical progress,

Every Friday, mother and father, grandparents on both sides and Aunt Thérèse - my dear spinster aunt, alas deceased now, who had spent her life as a feared barrister, the very one who broke the heart of several married and unmarried colleagues of hers and of others, many residents of our little town - have season tickets for the evening concert at our local Philharmonic.

On Sunday morning, mother, father and I go to the matinée of the same Philharmonic as my parents want me to acquire a refined musical education.

I do not want to spend every Sunday morning sitting in a chair smelling of moth balls, when I can listen to the play on the wireless.

'The Rite of Spring is a great piece, you'll enjoy it. It's for young people like you.' My father informs me as he is buttoning his coat.

'Pull your knee socks, Adèle.' Says my mother who is keen on minute detail.

I pretend to do just that, but I stroke the tomcat instead.

We walk to the concert hall. It is two short streets away, right in the centre, opposite the Baroque Town Hall.

I hate the ritual. I hate these concerts meant to enhance my education! I hate the Philharmonic and its conductor, the uncle of one of my primary school colleagues! I hate classical music! Every Sunday morning!

We get there and sit on our usual chairs in the front row.

The conductor raises the baton for the opening bars. The high bassoon sounds like a storm in my brain and I cannot help but pound out the rhythm with my fists on the arms of the

chair. The conductor turns and looks straight at me. I feel my parents' palms on both sides trying to restrain me. I move my head left then right and I cannot understand why their faces look ecstatic.

My mother shuffles a folded piece of paper into my hands. After spending a whole summer reading daily with mother's father, I am able to read fluently,

The Programme informs me that there are two parts to this concert:

I. The Adoration of the Earth

II. The Sacrifice

What follows is hitting me like a hammer. Each part has thirteen more or less continuous movements with folk-like fragments of melody. It might be I am not good at understanding the written word. It cannot be true!

The woodwind instruments follow loud in my ears; they do my head in with trills and arpeggios. Then it goes worse, there is a lone bassoon. Stamping violins, then the barks of eight horns make me jump in my seat. The music digs deep furrows onto my grey matter!

'How long will it last?' I ask my father in a loud voice.

He discreetly places a finger over his mouth as the conductor turns towards the audience and arrows me again. My father smiles.

Two bass tubas followed by outburst timpani, two piccolo flutes and a high piccolo set a rhythm that makes me want to scratch my arms and my legs. I cannot help it! Mum is holding my hand. I am trying to break free.

Strings, followed by the bass drum, and timpani centre-stage. The sound of wild hunting calls from the first two horns make me burst into a loud laughter. What comes next is quiet trilling flutes that bring my laughter into the open.

The conductor stops the music, turns to the full house and, in no bit about the bush words, utters in a thundery voice:

'Remove that child from the auditorium at once!'

Before my parents can intervene, I stand up and say with no trace of emotion the first thing that comes into my head,

'I am here to acquire a musical education!'

The conductor resumes the concert. My feet move in the rhythm of the music with the horns and then with the flutes, followed by the large gong and the trombone. It is all energy, trombones, tubas and timpani.

I am now scratching the arm rests during the percussive theme and the fanfare motif played by the horns and by me humming, though not in tune. It reminds me of the revving of a motorbike. Tubas are bellowing, the high piccolo trumpet keeps screaming out.

It deafens me!

Momentary silence, except for my humming. It does not make any difference. I feel the end is in view!

The solo strings are followed by a seismic bass drum, timpani and basses. Then this frenzied music - I don't want to listen to - stops abruptly.

I stand up and run out of the auditorium before the conductor has the time to bow to the audience, who all are watching me now!

My parents follow me in a measured step.

'Stop looking at me! I am going home now!' I tell them decisively. 'I am not staying through part two! It's all so horrid!'

'You are early!' I can hear the part-time gardener from behind the raspberry bushes.

'The orchestra was not up to it, Mr. Ensilage.'

Mother-in-law is now very vivid and at her third triple whisky. I decline another double. She informs me she is going to tell me a secret. I explain to her that a secret is private and confidential and not to be repeated, but she insists that, as I am her confidant, she sees no problem there. It's about Mafalda, our eldest daughter. It goes as follows,

Did the washing and put it in the tumble dryer – tick

Did the washing up in the dish washer – tick

Did sort out the beds – tick

I had to do all this as our nanny is on holiday and Bunny is over to New York on business for his bank.

Daily talk on the phone with mother – tick

Over-extensive talk on the mobile with Jamie, my secret of secrets – tick.

I could have done some work in the garden, but decided not to as our part-time gardener complained of my latest intervention. Instead, I walked our gun dogs twice, parasol and sunhat included. The gun dogs are becoming more boisterous by the day, as experienced by Bunny's bespoke handmade furniture, the imprint of their teeth carved in bas-relief everywhere.

I shall make a cup of Sumatra coffee, ground it myself and open all the doors to let the aroma spread all over the house.

I am waiting for the youngest to come home from the junior school round the corner. The other three are in Switzerland on a trip in the mountains with their boarding school masters.

I sit down contemplating the front garden with its very parched lawn and cockerel shaped topiary on two sides. Money well spent on the part-time gardener and his full-time assistant on work experience.

I am thinking of Jamie. I couldn't see him this morning as he had to go to London for the filming of another episode. I wonder if our youngest is a Jamie's indiscretion. Bunny and Jamie are pretty close in appearance.

I sip from my cup of coffee. All is quiet in our home of dreams. The stillness is punctuated by the gundogs' gnawing at the legs of one of the mahogany chairs in the kitchen. A hover-fly is fighting with the window frame. I open the triple glazed window.

I can hear a primordial noise shatter the peace of the afternoon. My heart is in my throat and the hairs on my arm stand to attention. I am all eyes but I cannot see anything, so I get the binoculars. I look at ground level, then in the air. A black wave as far as the eyes can see is crisscrossing the sky, covering the sun and the blue of the afternoon.

The gundogs are whining like when they are at the vet's.

I close the window downstairs and run upstairs to check if they are also closed.

I go downstairs, though by now I am shaking and I am out of breath.

I look out and see hundreds, perhaps thousands of ravens landing on our lawn, on the topiary, in the ancient oak trees that came with the land. I can hear their deep squawks.

And our youngest will soon be back from school. Think, think, what would Bunny do? Probably nothing. I gingerly open the front door, but it's blocked by the birds.

I get my mobile and I call the school. There is no answer. I call 999 and ask for the fire brigade. I tell them the reason. At the other end, a female voice informs me that our bespoke postcard village has been invaded by ravens and their advice is to stay inside our homes until further notice. I explain to this voice that I need to collect my child from school. She advises me to remain indoors and she tells me that all the public buildings have been informed and asked to keep doors and windows closed and wait for further instructions as the army has been called.

Well, well, well, our prim and proper Mafalda, just imagine! I shall not repeat this to Myfanwy as she is going to go ballistic, for a week at least.

Made my way home, made a cup of tea and a sandwich. Went to bed immediately.

*Monday yet again*

Mother-in-law had Mrs Gregson, her best friend for elevenses. They had a frank discussion about their neighbours, Stella the banker and her house husband. They do not have children yet as Stella is still following a bright career in investments and must travel a lot to the Continent.

'Perfect!' He gets his keys and almost like a teenager he rushes over the gravel of the drive. He trips over and steadies himself in Stella's climbing roses.

'Bother!' and he sucks his right hand middle finger.

He opens the door of the Porsche and he is off.

It's a boys' night out at the Club. He cannot wait to lose himself on the dance floor.

Before the clock strikes midnight, he takes his leave and accelerates home He arrives in time, takes a quick shower and puts his shirt, socks and underwear in the washing machine. When Stella enters the house, he is in the living room, a book open upside down.

'What a rotten evening I had!' she puffs and huffs, 'I see you finished the house chores.'

'I had a most rewarding evening. First the ironing, then an improving book.' He answers lost in reverie.

'I am off to bed. An early start at the office tomorrow!' and she goes to the bathroom and bolts the door.

'Another cup of tea?'

'Yes please!'

'You see', mother-in-law sips from her China cup of tea with willow prints, 'I don't know what's going on next door. Last night after she left, he got his new car out of the garage and was off. I am almost sure he has a fancy woman. Just imagine it!'

'As soon as the wife is out of the house... Cannot trust them nowadays! It really does go to show that young lasses nowadays are too free-spirited and one might even utter, though highly politically incorrect, that feminism has gone to their heads.' Utters Mrs Gregson.

'Correct. They lack discretion. Another cup of tea?'

'No thank you. I am off to the reading group at the library. Keep me posted on any new developments with next door.'

Back from the office, Stella slumps herself into the armchair and takes her high heel shoes off.

'What a day I had! Two conferences and the new interns are a nightmare!'

'We need to talk, Stella!'

'Not now! Can't you see how exhausted I am?'

'It will not wait, Stella! It's pressing!'

'Well, how to put it, Stella?'

'Yes?...'

'Well I'd like to take a cruise round the world'

'Well, if this makes you happy. It does interfere with our domestic arrangements! Who's going to look after the house here?'

'You'll need to advertise, I shall be away for several months.'

'What would the neighbours say? Especially the bat next door!'

'Another cup of tea?'

'Yes, please. How are your neighbours? I haven't seen him for a couple of months. I used to see him on Friday market like clockwork.' Says Mrs Gregson.

'Well, there have been some developments there...'

'What? What?'

'He went away, not sure why. She told me over the fence while our maid was collecting the washing the other day. He went on a cruise, round the world. I believe he left her!'
'How long will he stay there?'
'It really isn't that hard to understand, after all, she'd established all these rules and regulations he couldn't face! No wonder he left her.'

Stella is back from the office.
What a day I had! I am so looking forward to the weekend! This sustainability issue is doing my head in! She rubs her feet liberated from a brand new pair of very high-heel shoes.
Someone is knocking at the front door. This is the time she misses Rupert the most. The domestic she hired by the hour does the jobs and is off to another client.
She wobbles to the front door.
Stella's eyebrows lift in a question mark, like a painted leech.
'Hi, Stella! Don't you recognise me? It's me Rupert! I am back! Never again, It was a torture. No matter what tablets I took I was as seasick as a parrot, all the time. Even when the sea or the ocean was as flat as a mirror!'
Stella pulls him in. She does not want Mrs Gregson to hear this, as she is such a gossip.
'I can't tell you how glad I am. Still OK for our domestic arrangements?'
'Without a shadow of a doubt, Stella!'

'Another cup of tea?'
'Yes, please. What's going on with your neighbour?'
'Well, she's not so rushed off her feet at the moment. She's got a new man staying with her. He looks very much like her old husband, but more suntanned and slender, though two peas in a pod!'

Back from mother-in-law's and her gossip. Preparing dinner for Myfanwy and I. A great treat!

*Friday, gardening day*

Joanne and Tim, our new neighbours worry me. Mother-in-law drew my attention the other day as to Tim's obsessive activity in their garden. Yesterday Joanne had elevenses with mother-in-law and was able - at mother-in-law's subtle persuasion - to get Tim's odd behaviour off her chest.

Joanne cannot sleep since Tim has started another one of his well-planned holes. Her gaze floats from behind the damask curtains of her bedroom over the maze of little pegs with which he has marked his trench since dawn.

From her bedroom window, Joanne ventures a loud,

'What are you up to over there, old git?'

Tim ignores her and his spade becomes a dipping and rising oar.

'I'm getting there! Plodding, that's the secret!' He whistles to himself.

Tim digs deep into the soil and some clods slither, others prowl, but most of them fly.

Joanne can see the spade like a flashlight carving deep into the ground. The aged beast has kept her awake from her siesta yet again.

When he draws his breath, Tim steals a look at the carved stones of the cottage suffocated in climbing roses. Tim hates their smell, but has always put on a pretence mask on the topic of Joanne's roses.

'I'm getting there! Plodding, that's the secret!'

Sweat carves arches and columns over his face and his chest is under the shock of rising and falling tides.

Tim digs deep in the hope of reaching the gilded barge in which he could cross the silver sea.

'I am getting there! Plodding, that's the secret!'

Tim can almost see his city of dreams, enveloped in banners pulled taut by the breeze. The image vaults and multiplies into a myriad of other images.

Joanne's X-rays gaze measures the hole from her Juliet's hide. Tim stumbles over the paving stones of the path and into the hole.

Mother-in-law thought Tim's behaviour 'different', though what's happening in his garden is his own business. After all, he does not have pets to dig my bulbs like Mrs Gregson's new neighbours. Mrs Gregson has been mother-in-law's confidante since boarding school. This is what has happened to her recently, as recounted by mother-in-law.

'Anyway, you see…What I want to say…' utters Mrs Gregson

'What, what? Mother-in-law traces her hand over her drum stretched skin.

'Anyway, you see… I am concerned my dear husband has taken to working in the garden on a grand scale.'

'You don't say! You don't say!' Mother-in-law explores her cosmetically enhanced haunted nose.

'Anyway, you see…He never showed any interest in our garden until this summer!' says Mrs Gregson.

'What? What?' mother-in-law readjusts her ocean pearls over her hanging double chins.

'Anyway, you see…to tell you the truth, he's out with the lark – before and after work!' whispers Mrs Gregson.

'How's that? How's that?' Mother-in-law echoes her fingers into her highlighted glorious hair.

'Anyway, you see…He stopped going to the pub altogether. He's either in the garden in daylight or in the spare bedroom on his exerciser or on the bike' complains Mrs Gregson.

'Really? Really?' Mother-in-law rubs her nose in anticipation.

'He has pruned all the bushes, he has shortened all the trees…and it's not even the season!' reveals Mrs Gregson.

'True! True!' My in-law smiles with wrinkled lips.

'Anyway, you see! I was just cleaning the windows of the spare room, where my dear husband exercises now, the one facing the new neighbour…confesses Mrs Gregson.

'Which one? Which one?' My in-law splendour in winter's eyes pin her gaze.

'You know, the one who moved into Sally's place…the one with the two Dalmatians and the rescued horses…Sally who is romancing the young vet! Informs Mrs Gregson.

'I know now who you mean! I know now who you mean!' My in-law twitters on the parched texture of her skin.

'Well, I could not believe my eyes! I got his binoculars that were handy on the window sill…The new neighbour…the peroxide blonde lass was there spread on the lawn, our little Tibbs spread near her blood shot painted nails! Her head was hidden behind a wide straw hat. The rest was uninhibited skin, exposed to the sun! Can you imagine that?' and Mrs Gregson blushes with embarrassment.

'Well, well, call me old-fashioned, but I would have thought by now, with all the images on the TV and the internet, you should not look so shocked!' concludes mother-in-law.

After all these details I left mother-in-law to watch the evening news. She has become the barometer of the street. What she does not know, it's not worth knowing.

*Thursday, shopping day*

Dip, said mother-in-law, take a look at this photograph. I was getting ready for my big day! My first day at boarding school! I can visualize it as if it were yesterday. Or today! I was facing out to my future. I was about to start my education against my will. Maman had decided and that was that. She was like an admiral on a sailing ship gliding me on the ocean of life. I was off to that Boarding High-School for Little Witches, as all my colleagues called it! I had a horrible time, though it was my making. I acquired a good accent, the result of many elocution lessons and I bagged a rich and well-connected husband in your father-in-law! I remember the re-occurring nightmare of trying to escape from this Boarding High-School for Little Witches. After so many years, once again, I had this nightmare last night!

'Then, it's settled.' I could barely hear maman's soft honey-like voice.

'Do' know! Do' want to go! I want to stay at home! With Gran!' and I began to scream and frantically thump my feet on the Persian carpet, one of maman's more substantial dowry pieces, which has escaped the many types of moths so active in summer.

'You have to go there, Adèle! What will the relatives say! Every young girl in our family went to a finishing school to become a lady.'

'Don't want to become a lady. I wan' to stay at home with Gran!'

'Well, we'll see about that, in a day or two.' And maman took her bespoke handbag and left the room to go into town.

I ran into the garden to find Gran eating cherries directly from one of our cherry trees. Sob...sob...sob... Gran took me in her arms and pressed me to her ample bosom.

'Here. Have my good luck silver coin.' That calmed me down.

'Have you been to a boarding school, Gran?' I asked her, hoping she'll say NO. Sob...sob...sob...

My 'Ides of March' came soon enough for me. The reality sank in when maman asked Gran,

'Will you please sit on the case, so we can close it!'

The following morning the air was agitated by weeping leaves and furious branches. Maman shuffled me, my face doubled in size by a whole night of tantrums and screaming, into our barouche. Our magic horses took off and from there we reached the Boarding High-School for Little Witches in the blink of an eye.

Maman pulled me out of the barouche. Maman got my case off and pushed me onto the high steps of a bunker-like building. A Darwinian specimen appeared at the door, and said,

'You are late!'

Before I could reply, she levitated my case, as maman and our barouche disappeared like a whisper into the late summer air.

I was still wiping my tears, as I glided sucked into the inside of the building. Captured, I felt moving against my will along a corridor of mirrors with no reflections. I was placed in a classroom of sixty-six girls, all about my age.

I sat at the front at the only empty desk I could find.

As I was crumpled with grief, the door opened in thunder.

Two wrinkled teachers dressed in haute couture deux pièces and waxed faces came in.

There was the silence of the dark matter in the classroom. The teacher with the teeth like machetes, the hair a fire beehive and a dressmaker's ruler in the right hand thundered:

'I am the headmistress of this Boarding High School of rural excellence. This is my secretary. You will obey and learn to become genuine ladies. Let's see the length of your skirts.'

She went on from one girl to another and measured the length of each dress as her secretary made notes in a notebook.

Then she screamed with the voice of a tuba. One could see her tongue as sharp as a lemon over deep wounds.

'Girl, you've got your hair died in flame colours. That's my colour and no one is allowed to replicate it! And your eyebrows have been plucked!' The unlucky girl started to sob a clouded explanation, but no one was listening.

'Do something about this during the break! Or else!' She said this and left the classroom in a silent amount of personal curses.

At break I approached the girl, who appeared stunned.

'Do you want to get out of here? I do!'

Trembling, she just nodded. I took her by the hand and we began exploring the corridor.

'Let's pretend we need to use the facilities. Just in case someone asks!'

We walked to the end of the corridor, with displays of little witches and their brooms in graduation attire. At the end of the corridor, we ran down a staircase which led to an unlocked door.

From there, we could see the back gate, slightly ajar, with not a guard in sight. We slid out and we found ourselves in a narrow alley at the back of some bungalows. We began to run towards a wooded area we spied at the end of the alley. The trees were loaded with sleeping ravens.

I whispered to my shivering colleague.

'Have you got a comb or a brush on you?'

She did not reply, but she pulled her hair net and handed it to me. I checked inside my pockets. I had my good luck silver coin and a milk tooth.

When we reached the end of the alley, a siren noise burst out from the direction of the Boarding High School for Little Witches, which in turn woke up the army of ravens. They were now flying close to us in increasing numbers.

I threw the hair net in their direction; though I could not remember the spell I often heard the women in my family use.

We ran like stiches in a pattern inside the wooded area, where the ravens could not spread their wings across.

'It worked this time, let's hurry!' I said. She just nodded and we were making progress.

Not long, we heard behind us,

'I shall get you, make no mistake!' Our hunter was close by.

I threw my milk tooth and a wall higher than the Great Wall of China rose behind us.

We were almost running out of breath, when we spotted the secretary of the headmistress witch in the air, on a broom of thunder.

I took my good luck silver coin and threw it in the air.

I woke up in my bed. All sweaty, Gran near me, gently shaking me and maman softly whispering in my ear:

'You had a bad dream, darling! Do not worry, darling!'

I reassured mother-in-law that it was just a nightmare and that she should not read anything into it. In my opinion, which I kept to myself, she is indulging in too many glasses! She needs a new hobby to distract her from all this intensive gossip!

*Tuesday, small market day*

It was before 7.00am when they called me from the station as they are short staffed because one of my colleagues had to sort out the exchange student her son offered to host. The story went round the station as follows,

'I am going to show you the sights of our compact... but beautiful little town!' utters our guide.

'It looks compact...I understand. A Market Place in the old town... deserted! Empty streets... guarded by lamps with built up piles of bird droppings underneath...heaps! Well what can I say?' and Luc leans over to Jean, his best friend.

'Umm?...It's a country of animal lovers...But beautiful!...I say!...

No high buildings.' Replies Jean, dragging his Converse on the broken tarmac.

'They are all flat! They're obsessed with red bricks! I say! Are all these houses cloned? Not a bit of concrete anywhere!'

They follow the guide, all twenty or so of them, all from the L'Isle de Rée area, on the Atlantic coast.

'Some are made of stacked stones...'

Luc checks his smart phone and points ahead '...and the mud under my trainers! Oh là là là!...What would pauvre maman say? Umm?...'

Jean looks at Luc in amazement. 'Good country landscape! Good country food!'

'Jean, you are deluded! On the contrary! Look at me! I am a shadow of myself! You might have been lucky with your hosts! As for me! Day in and day out…salad and sandwiches…tomato sandwiches, cucumber sandwiches, red pepper sandwiches. The salads? Umm? Well! It's tomato or cucumber, or both, sometimes with onions and an awful lot of lettuce. No vinaigrette. Nothing!'

'You are so fussy, Luc! It's week days! I asked my host: "Do you ever cook?" She looked at me sort of taken by surprise and replied sort of flustered "Ah! That happens on Sundays!" But…There is no evidence of it yet! Sis Aurélie warned me, "Luc, ils ne cuisinent jamais! C'est affreux !" What will pauvre maman say to that? Umm? Take breakfast for example. Cereals and …Cereals day in and day out! I want confiture like maman makes from abricots every late spring.'

'Luc, how you exaggerate, my friend! Lunch surely is …'

'Jean you guessed…packed, you guessed, it's sandwiches variés.

'Luc, then dîner it's…'

'Don't hold your breath…it's sandwiches avec répétition. The folk here surely like to graze! What will pauvre maman say to that? Umm?…'

'Luc, it's not that bad!…You get used to it!…'

'Jean, you might think so! Just remember the Sunday trip, with my new and beaux trainers, size 10; after that voyage terrifiant at Cley in the rain and mud, heaps of it, to see the seals, my trainers have turned size12 now! I look like a March hare! The ride in le bateau open, no cover …Was effrayant!  All of us were screaming!'

'Luc, we were excited!'

'Jean, you are deluded! Really? One girl in particular, with coloured braces…'

'So, Luc?'

'She got on my nerves. I applied some freshly chewed gum to her hair and, when the teachers were not looking, I pinched her!'

'Luc, why did you do it?'

'I had to do it, Jean! To give her reason for deafening me with her hysterical screaming! She accused me, and the teacher being on her side, sanctioned me with a letter home! After all I had to put up with!'

'Surely, it's not so bad, Luc!'

'It is, it is…remember when we arrived in London and had to catch the Norwich train? We were all sitting in our seats when M. Bonnard realised he had left his back pack at the station café and he had to run for it, with minutes to spare because the station police had been alerted and they were on their way to destroy it. We all anticipated he would not catch the train, but he boarded it as it was about to leave the platform.'

'Our M. Bonnard, has an obsession with visiting country homes. He keeps saying that history made this country! What will pauvre maman say to that? Umm?'

'Well, Luc…It's all educational!'

'Jean, what about the weather? Every day… my host sits in front of the TV glued to the weather forecast. As if it matters! Il pleut every day, forecast or no forecast. The plus is, they do not have indoor pets, otherwise I'll have to share my bed with them! I rest my case! What will pauvre maman say to that? Umm?...'

'It's a school exchange, Luc! It will be the making of us, as M. Bonnard keeps saying!'

'Isn't he just! He does not live with my hosts!'

I am glad our children are grown up now and in charge of their own fate! I shall have that salad after all! In front of the TV, of course!

*Friday, extended market day*

My sister, who is a journalist, has two lovely daughters, Fiametta and Bianca. Everybody says so, those who are not directly connected to them or to our immediate family.

'Of course you can't keep it! You've got to give it back NOW or the consequences could be, well mum will give you a good telling off and they won't take you with us to Gran on Christmas day.' Says Bianca.

'You, horrible, horrible sister, I have not taken it and you know it! You are always making things up! You heard what Uncle Dip said when he visited us with Aunt Myfanwy last weekend! He said you were really, really awful!' replies Fiametta.

'Give it back or you'll suffer the consequences!'

'Like what, Bianca? Stop menacing! Mum…Mum…'

'See, see, she is not coming to your rescue, Fiametta! You are always driving her mad! Besides, she was in a hurry to go out! So there! Nobody can hear you NOW! I want it!'

'With these scissors, I shall cut, cut, cut!'

'No, please, no, Bianca! I'll let you use my jewellery box. But please, do not cut! No! Mum! Mum!'

'What's going on? Can't you see that I am busy? What have you done now?'

'Mum, mum, Bianca's cutting Copernicus' fur, mum! Come quickly upstairs!'

'That better be good!…What have you done?'

'Ouch! It has scratched me! It hurts! Mum, mum…'

'I told you not to bother my rabbit, Bianca! And I promised to let her use my jewellery box, but she wouldn't give it up! It serves you right!'

'I cannot get two minutes of peace and quiet in this house! I don't know! You two!'.

I don't live with them so I count my blessings.

*Saturday morning*

Mother-in-law asked me to accompany her for constitution walk in the countryside. She recalled how father-in-law bought two gundogs many years ago. Though he never did any shooting.

'It's your turn to take the gun dogs for a walk in the park.'

'You should not have bought these gun dogs, Peregrine.'

'I had to, Adèle, to match my Purdy guns.'

'But you never hunt, Peregrine.'

'It makes a good impression with the clients at the bank, the mahogany case with the guns and the picture of the gun dogs above on the wall.

I put my wellingtons and take the animals by their leads. Out of the kitchen door. Across the street and we are in the park

and along the Serpentine with whispering willows. The fragrance of the freshly cut grass bounces into the nostrils of the dogs and agitates them. In the grass, daffodils have almost opened amongst glimpses of the dying dew. The trot of a lonely rider dilutes into the distance, flushing a flock of ravens, surreal over the mirror of the water. The dense scaffold of trees rises on one side of the path. I let the dogs free and I stop on a bench by the lake.

Fumes break loose from it and I can see Tommy in my secret dream of dreams.

Alas, Tommy and I first embraced behind the bike sheds at the middle school amongst the autumn leaves during intense rehearsals for the Harvest Festival.

We kissed again behind the tractor working deep furrows on my uncle's field of garlic wedged between the old village hall and our school. Then, suddenly, the sky lit with fireballs, explosions of the heart followed by erosions chiselled in by our teacher's scream from the first floor window of our classroom.

At that moment in time mummy and daddy moved me to a private school.

Tommy and I never kissed in Independence Square as the storm swayed, and the rain squeezed me against the cast-iron railings and the bushes.

Tommy was on a tandem on the express lane, I was on my journey to nowhere at the corner.

Random flashes. Light needles of rain intrude my pain.

Cranes are hovering above in the sky. The gun dogs are nowhere to be seen. I get the whistle out. Three distinctive shapes are gaining ground, tails wagging and a young duck in each mouth.

'You rotten boys!' I can hear my voice a menacing needle.

They reach me and they sit and wait for me to put their leads on. There is stillness in the air. Sculptured trees follow the path. We exit the park and cross the street.

We enter our house by the back door.

I leave the gun dogs in the conservatory, which Peregrine likes to call his Orangerie, though we haven't got one living plant in it.

'Hi Peregrine, your gun dogs…'

We walked about three miles, which is mother-in-law's distance limit. On the other hand, I walk 20 km once a week with Jimmy, my colleague from the station and I exercise at home daily.

*Wednesday, a free day*

Over elevenses, mother-in-law told me about her former music education. She has a grand piano in their music room, but I never heard anybody play it. As a young lass, my mother-in-law had issues with her piano lessons,
'Look at the music, think of the keys and only after that you press the key, when you're completely certain!'
My teacher twists her fingers in a knitted pattern and jumps them over her sleeves the way a squirrel I saw in the municipal park does.
A whimpering sound comes out of the keys first, then a howling one.'
'No, no, and no. That will not do. It's a Lullaby. Andante, dear. Not Allegretto. It's not a dance.'
Her eyes have an appointment with the ceiling and then she moves her head from left to right or is it the other way.
I can sense she is about to work herself out into a frenzy.
I dare a 'would you please, Miss, play it to me as an example first.'
She does not wait to be asked a second time, she sets herself straight at the piano and lets her fingers go. The music comes to life as she plays. I watch what she does like a hawk, though I do not listen to the music. To remember what she does comes easy to me. Grandma pointed out to me this very
morning, 'ask your teacher to play it first and then your memory will register everything.'
It's my turn now and I can play it exactly, though I pretend to look at the music. Mother and father take me to the matinée concerts to our local Philharmonic. During the concert, I keep moving my feet like a see-saw. I don't understand why the person in the seat in front of me turns and gives me some frosty looks. I kicked the front seat only a few times.
Now I have quite a repertoire and my father who is in charge of my musical education has been invited to check my progress.
'She is full of promise' utters my father proudly.
All goes according to plan until my music teacher has the uninspired idea to ask me to play a new piece.
'Could you please play it first, Miss?'

'Well, try it on your own for a change.' My fingers clutch at the keys. My mind is blank and all is night and darkness in front of my eyes. I feel like a clipped hedge and very tempted to run away.

'You can do it, Adèle.' My father encourages me.

I know differently. I can read the music. I know the keys, but I cannot put them together.

My music teacher plays the piece, just to save the day. She knows she wants the money for the lesson; I know that as she always asks for it before I even sit down.

I play the piece too and without fault.

On the way home, I tell my father,

'I don't want to go to my music lesson any longer.'

'Why is that? You are playing well.'

'I cannot read and play the music at the same time, daddy.'

'We'll have to see what mummy will decide, OK?'

I kept my eyes closed during her story. I returned home, put a CD on and made myself a drink. I see that Myfanwy is still busy at the Chambers.

# The Old Police House

'He will never go…never…' These images were stencilled in my mind as I tried to pour light over the fissured world of my mother's.

My thoughts echoed the sounds of the fast train. It was slicing between twisted rocks. The day rustled with the short horizon. Stamping thoughts kept invading my mind again and again. I was sitting in the middle seat of a second-class compartment.

I was returning from the reading of my mother's will. I learnt from the solicitor, whose chambers I had attended before eleven, that my mother had left me the old police house built in the Dutch style.

I had walked to the house before taking the train back. I wanted to see it once again. It was a steep climb as the little town had been built on the slopes of a hill. I found the house engulfed by the whispers of the oak trees, as the dusk was hovering over its crumbling masonry, now patterned in ivy. One of its chimneys was missing. The windows had their shutters closed.

I dared not unlock the front door. Instead, I walked away along the hedges that were casting shadows onto the waters of the river. Faint lights were being born on the other side. Willows were hiding their thinness in the dimming light. The smell of burning coal was wafting from barges.

I made it to the railway station with a few minutes to spare. I could sense him. He was there waiting for me to come closer. He stared at me in the silence of the platform. I felt his eyes hurting inside me. My lips felt tight. I was numb.

Passengers boarded the train and the intercity gained speed.

Images of the old police house with the Dutch gable disturbed my thoughts. From the middle seat of the second-class compartment, the journey made me daydream… a young girl walking along the blue sands built in little forts on the shore of the river…jumping over rigid lumps of driftwood… resting on the shore…

Our old police house, with its wrought-iron lamp holder in the shape of a laughing lizard stood amongst pig squeals and odour of fresh manure. I could see the drawing room with oak shutters that opened like the wings of a raven, the silent parquet flooring and the hand-printed wallpaper. They were all there. The boudoir grand piano. The mirror with a carved bird on top. The pike holding a tiny fish in its teeth, mounted amongst rocks and reeds in a bow-fronted glass case placed on the mantelpiece. The wooden two-story dolls house with a cockerel weather vane. The expanded body of an old Jack-in-the-box that made me jump when it erupted in spasms. From above the fireplace, the life-size painting of a young man dressed in blue and wearing tennis shoes, who always seemed to follow me wherever I was in the drawing room.

I would tell mother, 'His eyes are following me, mum! I don't like him! I want to go back to our other home!'

'Nonsense!' Mother would reply.

I would tell Mother of the scales and arpeggios I could hear played on the grand piano of the drawing room, but Mother kept saying, 'It's your tinnitus playing you up again!'

Or I would complain, 'Mum, listen! I had nightmares last night! I felt heavy weights on my chest!

Mother would look at me pensively and utter in her softest tone, 'Nonsense! It's nerves before your mock-exams! There's a perfectly good explanation!

'I want to go back to our home, Mum! To my friends! I don't want to live in this house!'

'This is a period house surrounded by an arboretum. It's a rara avis! Just look at the view!'

At the summer solstice, mother had to work at the pharmacy in the afternoon. As I came back from school, I could hear tractors at work in the fields and I could see the local flock of ravens flush over. I could feel the mist break loose through the oak trees. I put the key in and pressed the brass handle.

Behind the door, I could about see the silhouette of a young man dressed in blue and wearing tennis shoes.

I could see myself hold tight to my Hessian bag. I tried to scream, but no sounds came out of my mouth. I ran down the hill for my life. I stopped only at the police station. There I uttered 'Help me, please!' and I collapsed on a chair.

'What seems to be the matter, Miss?' The sergeant on duty asked me.

'There is something going on inside our house.'

'Your address, Miss?'

'The old police house!'

'I thought it had been empty since I was a lad!' the sergeant replied.

'The man from the oil painting was at the door, when I opened it! We live alone, mum and I!'

They called mother from the pharmacy. That evening, I refused point blank to return to the house. Mother and I spent the night in the local hotel, where the receptionist was dressed in blue and wore tennis shoes.

I complained to mother of having felt heavy weights on my chest during the night and how I struggled to extract myself from sleep.

Mother replied in her soft voice, 'Nonsense! It's only your adolescence's insecurity!'

The following morning, we went to stay with relatives for a few days and I was packed off to a girls' boarding school.

The fast train was devouring my thoughts. Trees were galloping past the window. Through the window, the earth slapped me with shadows and grazing cows pounced through the view, choking my space.

My head leaned on his left shoulder and my eyes closed drifting.

'He will never go...never...not now anyway...

Printed in Poland
by Amazon Fulfillment
Poland Sp. z o.o., Wrocław